Little Rabbit waits for the moon

For Steph
B.S.

For Carla, Marshall and Liam
S.P.

First published in 2004
by Meadowside Children's Books
185 Fleet Street,
London EC4A 2HS

This edition published in 2008 by Little Bee
an imprint of Meadowside Children's Books

A CIP catalogue record for this book is available
from the British Library
Printed in Malaysia

10 9 8 7 6 5 4 3 2

Little Rabbit
waits for the
moon

little bee

Little Rabbit
couldn't sleep...

In the day,
the sun is there, warm
and bright. But when night comes,
the sky hangs low, dark and empty.

"If I fall asleep now, there'll be no one watching over me," thought Little Rabbit. "I'll just have to wait for the moon." And so he did just that.

The trouble with being
so tired and sleepy,
was that he didn't
know exactly when
the moon would come.

Little Rabbit waited
and waited.

More time passed
and the moon still
hadn't come.

He thought he had better ask
someone how much longer he
might have to wait.

"This is my first day, ever,"
said a small flower in the fields.
"Maybe I will have grown into a tree
by the time your moon comes."

That sounded like an awfully long time.

Little Rabbit thought he had better ask
someone else – just to be sure.

"Look deep into the water," shimmered a little lake nearby. "Maybe your moon has fallen in and can't get out."

That didn't sound like what he wanted to hear.

Little Rabbit thought he had better ask someone else – just to be sure.

"Why don't you walk with me?"
Twisted a long and winding path.
"We can find out where I'm leading
and maybe your moon is at the
other end!"

That sounded like it might
be a long way away.

Little Rabbit thought he had better ask
someone else – just to be sure.

"I've just blown in to these parts," breezed a wind that had picked up. "Who knows? I might be a big, fierce storm by the time your moon comes."

That didn't sound like something he wanted to wait for.

Little Rabbit thought he had better ask someone else – just to be sure.

"We can't see your moon yet," rumbled the great, rolling hills. "And we can see far into the distance from up here!"

That didn't sound very promising.

Little Rabbit began to think that the moon might never come. And he was getting awfully tired…

And then, from behind the hills,
carried by the wind along the twists
of the path, reflected in the lake, and shining
on the petals of the small flower…

...the most perfect moon
slid into the night sky.

But Little Rabbit

had fallen asleep, dreaming

of the moon that would

watch over him through the night.